TOP TRUMPS®

Hi, I'm Toppy!

And I'm Trumpy!

We're going to take you on a fun, fact-finding tour!

Creatures of the Deep

Explore the Ocean Depths!

Throughout this book, you'll discover all sorts of fascinating facts about the weird and wonderful creatures that live in the world's oceans. Plus there's lots of fun activities and cool new ways to play with your terrific Top Trumps cards!

An Undiscovered World
The deepest oceans are an incredible other world we know so little about. They are filled with huge killer whales and predatory sharks, but those are just the famous predators. As much as 99% of the world's habitable space is actually underwater, making the oceans and the creatures that live in them a huge part of life on Earth. But the seas are so deep that sunlight doesn't reach all the way down to the floor and both the pressure and darkness make exploration difficult. Who knows what could be lurking down there…!

An estimated 50-80% of all life on Earth is found under the ocean surface and the oceans contain 99% of the living space on the planet. Less than 10% of that space has been explored.

Earth's longest mountain range is the Mid-Ocean Ridge, which is more than 31,000 miles long. It is four times longer than the Andes, Rockies, and Himalayas combined!

Of all the plants and animals that exist, at least 85% of them live in the oceans and seas.

We have discovered 199,146 marine species so far, but scientists believe there could even be as many as 25 million species living in the oceans!

The Mariana Trench is the deepest known area of Earth's oceans. Located to the east of the Mariana Islands in the western Pacific Ocean, its deepest point is about 11,000 metres. That's equivalent to the height of Mount Everest, the highest mountain in the world!

GREAT WHITE SHARK

TOP TRUMPS

Size (cm)	600
Defences	49
Under Threat	3
Depth	62

Great Whites are one of the largest predators in the world, and their mouths contain over 300 serrated teeth!

What the Top Trumps Categories Mean

There are four different categories on each Top Trumps card – Size, Under Threat, Depth and Defences.

'Size' is the average length of an adult of the species in centimetres.

'Defences' – the higher the number, the better your creature is at defending itself.

'Under Threat' is measured using the IUCN Red List of Endangered Species, on a scale of 1 ('Least Concern') to 7 ('Extinct'). Remember, the LOWEST score wins on this category.

'Depth' – the higher the number, the deeper down in the ocean your creature can be found!

Just how big and how deep are the oceans?

1. Pacific Ocean
64,185,629 square miles
Greatest depth - 10,923m

2. Atlantic Ocean
33,424,006 square miles
Greatest depth - 9,219m

3. Indian Ocean
28,351,484 square miles
Greatest depth - 7,455m

4. Southern Ocean
13,513,576 square miles
Greatest depth - 7,236 m

5. Arctic Ocean
5,108,132 square miles
Greatest depth - 5,625m

70% of the Earth's surface is covered by oceans, the largest of which is the Pacific Ocean. It covers around 30% of the Earth's surface alone – in other words it's as big as all the land put together!

Despite their name, **seahorses** are actually fish. They breathe using gills and have a swim bladder to control their buoyancy. However, instead of having scales like most fish, a seahorse's body is covered in protective plates of bone.

Common Seahorse

COMMON SEAHORSE

TOP TRUMPS

Size (cm)	10
Defences	1
Under Threat	0
Depth	11

During mating season, seahorse eggs are carried by the males rather than females.

Hungry Horses
Seahorses are hungry fish! Because they don't have a stomach, the food passes through their bodies very quickly – which means they need to eat constantly!

Slow Swimmers
They might be fish, but seahorses are terrible swimmers. They prefer to rest in one area, sometimes holding on to the same coral or seaweed for days with their tails. When they do swim, they beat their fins very quickly (up to fifty times a second) but don't move very fast.

Did you know that, unlike any other species, male seahorses become pregnant?

1

How big?

Scientific name:
Hippocampus kuda

Eats
Shrimps and plankton

Where
Warm shallow waters all over the world

Lifespan
1–5 years

Predators
Crabs, Rays and Tuna

Although they spend a lot of their lives in the water, **common seals** are actually mammals. They breed, give birth to live young and nurse their offspring on the shoreline. Common seals are also known as Harbour Seals.

Common Seal

Seal Meals
Common seals have been known to attack, kill and eat some kinds of seabirds, but mainly feed on fish and squid. They find their prey by detecting vibrations in the water using their whiskers!

Predators and Pollution
Seals have several natural predators including sharks, orcas (killer whales) and polar bears, but the greatest threats to their lives are marine litter, pollution and the fatal phocine distemper virus.

COMMON SEAL

TOP TRUMPS

Size (cm)	185
Defences	12
Under Threat	1
Depth	79

Common Seals spend 85% of their day in the water; foraging for food, resting on the seafloor or drifting with sea currents.

Common Seal beats Common Sea Horse on Size, Defences, and Depth!

3

Well, did YOU know that the common seal can stay underwater for over twenty minutes?

Scientific name:
Phoca Vitulina

Eats
Fish and occasionally shrimps, crabs and squid

Where
Coastal waters of the northern Atlantic and Pacific oceans, the Baltic and North Seas

Lifespan
Twenty-five to thirty-five years

Predators
Killer whales, humans

How big?

Southern stingrays are experts at disguise! They have a diamond-shaped disc that is dark brown, grey or black on its upper side and white on the lower side. This helps them to camouflage themselves in the sand, where they spend most of their time.

Southern Stingray

SOUTHERN STINGRAY

TOP TRUMPS

Size (cm)	200
Defences	42
Under Threat	1
Depth	9

Stingray venom was once used by ancient Greek dentists as an anaesthetic!

Fishy Food
In some parts of the Caribbean it is possible to swim with stingrays and on the Turks and Caicos Islands they can be fed pieces of fish by hand!

Sting in the Tail
Southern stingrays have a long, whip-like tail with a barb at the end which they use for defence. They get their name from the sting in their tail, but they are much more likely to try to swim away if under threat than try to attack. The poison isn't fatal to humans but it can be incredibly painful.

Here's a great fact! All creatures produce an electrical field and stingrays can feel changes in them with their sensory nerves, helping them find their prey!

How big?

Scientific name
Dasyatis Americana

Where
Western Atlantic Ocean

Eats
Small crustaceans, worms and bony fish that live on the bottom of the sea

Predators
Large fish such as Hammerhead Sharks

Lifespan
Eighteen plus years

People often assume that **swordfish** use their long beak – or sword – to spear their prey, but in fact, they use it to slice away at their victims to make it easier to catch them. If they did spear their prey, it would only end up getting stuck on their beaks!

Swordfish

SWORDFISH

TOP TRUMPS

Size (cm)	200
Defences	48
Under Threat	1
Depth	10

Swordfish get their name from their long and pointy snout, but only use this "sword" in self-defence.

Night Feasts
Swordfish spend most of the daylight hours deep underwater and tend to come to the surface to feed at night. Swordfish are carnivores and eat other ocean fish such as bluefish, mackerel, hake, and herring as well as squid and octopus.

The Fastest Fish
Swordfish can swim at amazing speeds – up to sixty miles per hour. This makes them the speediest fish in the ocean.

2

This one's better! Swordfish can grow as much as 4.5 metres long – that's the length of a family car!

Swordfish beats Southern Stingray on Defences and Depth!

Scientific name
Xiphias gladius

Lifespan
Nine plus years

Predator
Humans are their most common predator

Where
Atlantic, Pacific and Indian Oceans

Eats
Fish that live near the surface of the sea

How big?

Gone Fishing

All of the creatures below can be found in the word grid – apart from one. Can you work out which one is missing?

A	F	I	S	H	A	R	K	B	R	P	A	K	H
N	I	F	H	T	T	A	B	R	A	P	U	H	R
I	S	F	S	T	I	N	G	R	A	Y	Y	A	R
H	H	H	T	T	W	C	A	F	H	R	B	A	A
P	P	G	U	I	A	R	N	I	P	G	R	B	A
L	E	E	S	W	O	R	D	F	I	S	H	A	P
O	N	L	N	G	U	I	F	B	R	B	C	R	E
D	G	T	P	E	N	C	R	I	P	S	H	C	N
B	A	R	C	R	E	D	I	P	S	P	O	T	S
P	B	U	G	N	I	B	G	R	C	H	P	I	S
G	E	T	N	G	E	P	U	F	F	G	A	M	H
C	L	P	E	M	A	N	A	T	E	E	E	R	E
P	O	W	C	L	O	W	N	F	I	S	H	E	K
C	P	L	P	W	P	E	A	G	I	P	S	H	A

STINGRAY

STARFISH

PENGUIN

SPIDERCRAB

SHARK

IGUANA

TURTLE

CLOWNFISH

MANATEE

SWORDFISH

DOLPHIN

HERMITCRAB

In Danger!

A person who studies the ocean is known as an **oceanographer**. A person who studies fish is called an **ichthyologist**. A person who studies other sea creatures is called a **marine biologist**.

Put these creatures of the deep in order of the threat they face of extinction. (Your Top Trumps cards will help you if you get stuck!)

☐ **LOGGERHEAD TURTLE**

☐ **ORCA WHALE**

☐ **IGUANA**

☐ **OCTOPUS**

☐ **MANTIS SHRIMP**

TOP TRUMPS MINI GAME

RANDOM CHOICE

This game is like normal Top Trumps – but with a twist. You don't get to pick the best category on your card, your opponent chooses a category without seeing your card. So, when Player 1 turns over his first card, he doesn't get to choose the category himself, Player 2 does instead! The player with the highest score in that category wins the round as usual. The winner then calls out a score on his next card, again with his opponent choosing the category first. The game continues like this until one person wins all the cards.

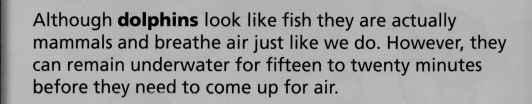

Although **dolphins** look like fish they are actually mammals and breathe air just like we do. However, they can remain underwater for fifteen to twenty minutes before they need to come up for air.

Bottlenose Dolphin

Finding Food
Dolphins can talk to each other by making clicks, squeaks and whistles. They can also locate food by making a clicking sound underwater and listening for the echo to tell whether or not there's something in the water with them. It's the same principle as a submarine's sonar system.

Water Source
Seawater is too salty for dolphins to drink, so although they live in the ocean, they live like desert animals with no direct source of drinkable water. Most of their water actually comes from their food (fish and squid).

BOTTLENOSE DOLPHIN

TOP TRUMPS

Size (cm)	366
Defences	0
Under Threat	1
Depth	59

Bottlenose Dolphins sleep with one side of their brain at a time, so that they can continue to swim to the surface to breathe.

Dolphins can't go to sleep like us, otherwise they would suffocate. Instead, they let half of their brain sleep at a time. Amazing!

3

Bottlenose Dolphin beats Loggerhead Turtle on Size, Depth and Under Threat!

How big?

Scientific name
Tursiops truncates

Eats
Small fish, crustaceans and squid

Lifespan
Can live for longer than forty years but the average seems closer to twenty

Predators
Large sharks

Where
Most oceans

Loggerhead turtles got their name because their oversized head resembles a big log. They have incredibly powerful jaws which they use for crushing prey with hard shells, such as conchs and horseshoe crabs.

Loggerhead Turtle

LOGGERHEAD TURTLE

TOP TRUMPS

Size (cm)	90
Defences	5
Under Threat	4
Depth	19

Almost a third of the world's Loggerhead Turtle population can be found off the beaches of Florida in the USA.

This one's INCREDIBLE! Loggerheads will swim a third of the way around the world in search of rich feeding grounds!

1

Turtles Under Threat
Once incredibly common, turtles have been an endangered species since 1978 – and not just because of natural predators. Their survival is also threatened by pollution, human activities in their nesting areas, and fishing nets.

Laying Eggs
A female loggerhead turtle nests every two-to-three years and travels thousands of miles to lay her eggs on the same beach where she hatched.

Scientific name
Caretta caretta and Caretta caretta gigas

Eats
Jellyfish, seaweed and shellfish

Where
Mediterranean (Carretta carretta) and Indian and Pacific Oceans (Caretta caretta gigas)

Lifespan
May live more than sixty-five years

Predators
Sharks, seals and killer whales when adult, but many more when young

How big?

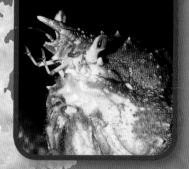

The **Japanese spider crab** is known as Takaashigani which means 'tall-footed crab' in Japanese. It has the largest leg span of any arthropod (a creature with jointed limbs) in the world, with a leg span of over four metres – that's the length of a family car!

Japanese Spider Crab

Spider Survivor
The Japanese spider crab is one of the longest-living creatures in the world, surviving up to 100 years!

Crabby Camouflage
To camouflage themselves against predators, young Japanese spider crabs attach sponges and other small marine animals to their shells, helping them blend in with the ocean floor.

Japanese Spider Crab beats Hermit Crab on Size, Defences and Depth!

JAPANESE SPIDER CRAB

TOP TRUMP

Size (cm)	440
Defences	14
Under Threat	1
Depth	100

Fully-grown Japanese Spider Crabs have a leg span of over four metres, and can live for 100 years!

3

Here's a fab fact . . . the Japanese spider crab has teeth – but like all crabs, its teeth are in its stomach!

How big?

Scientific name
Macrocheira kaempferi

Where
Near the coast of Japan

Lifespan
May live up to 100 years

Eats
Shellfish and animal carcasses

Predators
Octopuses and other large marine animals

Hermit crabs are different from most other crab species because they don't have a hard shell to protect their soft bodies. Instead, they find homes in the shells of other molluscs, and abandon them for bigger ones as they grow larger.

Hermit Crab

HERMIT CRAB

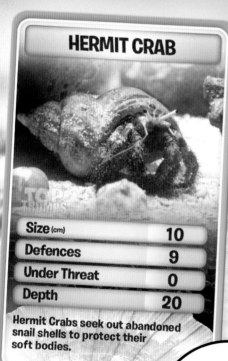

Size (cm)	10
Defences	9
Under Threat	0
Depth	20

Hermit Crabs seek out abandoned snail shells to protect their soft bodies.

This one's better! Hermit crabs take possession of empty shells. They don't kill the original occupants, but will sometimes encourage another crab to leave its shell by pulling it out!

1

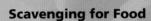

Scavenging for Food
Hermit crabs are scavengers. They are not particularly fussy eaters and will feed on whatever dead and decaying animals they find. If a hermit crab's shell is too small, the creature won't be able to retreat all the way into it, and so will be more vulnerable to predators.

Living Together
You might expect hermit crabs to live on their own, but they're not really hermits at all. They like a crowd and are often found in groups of 100 or more on the beach!

Scientific name
Paguroidea (family name) 100+ different species

Lifespan
Some have been known to live more than seventy years.

Eats
Almost anything, including small fish, worms, plankton and other food particles.

Predators
Humans pose the biggest threat as they like to collect the shells that hermit crabs need to live in.

Where
Deep ocean to rock pools

How big?

Spot The Difference

These underwater scenes may look quite similar, but there are actually ten differences between them. Can you find them all?

Shark Attack!

See if you can guide the Bottlenose Dolphin through the maze without it becoming shark food!

Keeping fish for pets began 4,500 years ago with the Sumerians, an ancient and advanced civilisation!

EXIT

TOP TRUMPS MINI GAME

HIDDEN DANGER

This is a game for two players plus another 'invisible' player.

STEP ONE

Shuffle your Top Trumps and deal them into three piles of six cards. Each player takes a pile and keeps it face down. The third pile is turned over and stays face up between the players.

STEP TWO

Player 1 picks a category. He looks at the topmost card in the middle and picks a category he hopes his card will beat. Both Player 1 and Player 2 turn over their top cards and see who has won.

STEP THREE

The winner takes all three cards and puts them at the bottom of their pile. Now it's Player 2's turn to choose the category. The game carries on until one of the three players has run out of cards.

The **basking shark** is the second largest fish on Earth after the whale shark. They generally grow to around 6-8 metres in length but the largest on record was 12 metres – longer than a double-decker bus! It might look scary, but the basking shark isn't an aggressive creature.

Basking Shark

BASKING SHARK

Size (cm)	800
Defences	18
Under Threat	3
Depth	8

Basking Sharks drift along the surface of the ocean, scooping up food in their large gaping mouths.

Filtering Food
The basking shark has five large gill slits on either side of its head which it uses to filter its food from the seawater as it swims. It can filter 1000 tonnes of water an hour – the equivalent weight of more than 150 African elephants!

Deep-Sea Divers
The sharks get their name from their habit of swimming along the ocean floor. Some basking sharks are incredible divers and have been spotted over 1,000 metres below the surface!

Did you know that despite its huge size, a basking shark has a very small brain? It's the size and shape of a hotdog in a bun!

How big?

Scientific name
Cetorhinus maximus

Where
Migrate all over the world

Lifespan
Not known

Predators
Killer Whales

Eats
Mainly plankton but also small fish and fish eggs

The **orca whale** is one of the ocean's top predators. They hunt all sorts of creatures – fish, seals, penguins, squid, sharks – even other kinds of whales! It's no surprise they're also called Killer Whales, but of the few recorded attacks on humans, none have been fatal.

Orca Whale

Orca Whale beats Basking Shark on Defences, Under Threat, and Depth!

ORCA WHALE

Size (cm)	800
Defences	41
Under Threat	0
Depth	42

Orcas travel and hunt in family "pods" of up to 40 whales, feeding off seals, fish and squid.

Well did YOU know that the largest male orca ever was 10 metres long and weighed 10,000 kg? About the size and weight of a double-decker bus!

3

Wolves of the Sea
The orca whale eats about 227kg of food a day – that's the combined weight of three men! It's also known as 'the Seawolf' because orcas hunt in packs like wolves. Their hunting techniques include grabbing seals straight off the ice, and also splashing their tails to make waves so penguins fall off ice floes!

Down in One
Orcas do not chew their food. They can swallow small seals and sea lions whole – the prey simply slides down the orcas' throats!

Scientific name
Orcinus orca

Eats
Fish, birds and other whales

Lifespan
Males live for an average twenty-nine years but females an average of fifty years

Where
All over the world

Predators
None. But sharks will prey on young, old or ill Orca Whales

How big?

The **common octopus** is one of the most intelligent creatures in the ocean. Each of its eight long arms has suckers on the underside. It uses these arms and suckers to catch and choke its prey.

Common Octopus

COMMON OCTOPUS

TOP TRUMPS

Size (cm)	60
Defences	8
Under Threat	2
Depth	52

The Common Octopus can change its skin colour to match its surroundings, helping it to hide from predators.

Boneless Body
There are no bones in an octopus's body. Their bodies are extremely flexible and can squeeze through incredibly small spaces.

Off the Scent
If under threat, an octopus can produce a cloud of black ink to hide its escape and affect its attacker's sense of smell. If an octopus loses an arm in a fight it doesn't have to worry. It can always grow another one!

I love this fact! An octopus has three hearts – two pump blood through the gills and the third pumps blood through the rest of its body!

How big?

Scientific name
Octopus vulgaris

Lifespan
Two years

Where
Mediterranean Sea, Eastern Atlantic ocean and off the coast of Japan

Eats
Crabs, crayfish and molluscs

Predators
Sharks, eels and dolphins

The monstrous-looking **angler fish** is not only one of the ugliest creatures on the planet, it lives in what is easily Earth's most inhospitable habitat – the bottom of the sea. No wonder it looks so unhappy!

Angler Fish

ANGLER FISH

TOP TRUMPS

Size (cm)	60
Defences	12
Under Threat	0
Depth	94

Angler Fish have an elongated spine which supports a special, light-producing organ - they use this as "bait" when hunting their prey.

Fishing for Prey
The angler fish gets its name from a growth that extends over its mouth like a fishing rod. The end glows to lure its prey towards it. It is able to stretch its jaw and stomach to swallow food that is twice its own size.

Sticking Together
A young male angler fish mates with a female by latching onto her with his sharp teeth. Over time, his skin sticks to her skin and their bloodstreams join. Eventually the poor angler fish loses his eyes and his internal organs. A female can carry six or more males at once!

Angler fish beats Common Octopus on Defences, Under Threat and Depth!

3

Mine's even better! The Angler fish's teeth point inwards to stop its prey escaping before it's finished eating them!

Scientific name
Members of the Lophiiformes family (there are more than 200 species)

Lifespan
Not known with any certainty

Eats
Other fish, even those twice its size!

Predators
Very few as long as they remain in deep water

Where
Worldwide

How big?

Finding Nemo

The Clownfish are hiding in the anemones.
How many can you count in the picture?

Ocean Floor

There are more species of fish in the oceans than there are all other species of mammals, reptiles, birds and amphibians combined!

Who swims there? Can you match the creature to the deep water they swim in? If you get stuck, use your Top Trumps cards to help you.

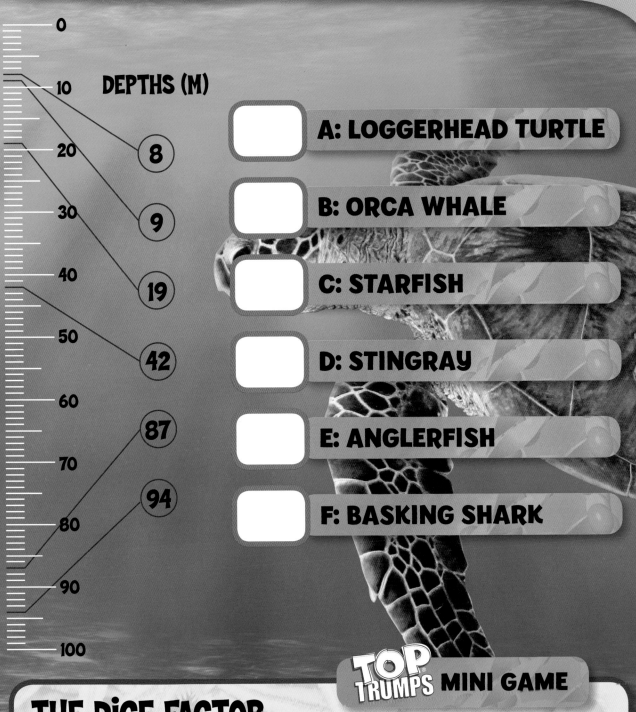

0

10 DEPTHS (M)

20   8

30   9

40   19

50

60   42

70   87

80   94

90

100

A: LOGGERHEAD TURTLE

B: ORCA WHALE

C: STARFISH

D: STINGRAY

E: ANGLERFISH

F: BASKING SHARK

TOP TRUMPS MINI GAME

THE DICE FACTOR

Players 1 and 2 play Top Trumps in the usual way. However, the game is also played with two dice to make things even more interesting! Player 1 reads out a category and score as normal, and Player 2 has to see if his score beats it. If Player 2's score is too low, he has a chance to increase it by rolling both of the dice and adding the total number to the score on his card. Play continues in the same way until one player wins all the cards!

Despite its name, starfish do not have gills, scales or fins or anything else that would make them fish. They are related to sea cucumbers and sea urchins. And although it's called a **crimson knobbed starfish**, this particular starfish is born green! It only turns red as it grows older.

Crimson Knobbed Starfish

Starfish Species
There are more than 1,600 species of starfish living in all the world's oceans. They live in every type of habitat, including tidal pools, rocky shores, sea grass, kelp beds, and coral reefs. Some even live in sands as deep as 9,000 metres.

Growing Back
Not only can a starfish grow a new limb if it loses one, it has been known for a severed limb to re-grow an entire starfish if it still has part of the centre attached!

CRIMSON KNOBBED STARFISH

TOP TRUMPS

Size (cm)	18
Defences	6
Under Threat	0
Depth	87

Starfish have the ability to re-grow parts of their body - so if they lose one of their arms, it can grow back!

Crimson Knobbed Starfish beats Clownfish on Size and Depth!

I'll bet you didn't know that a starfish has neither blood nor brains! Its 'blood' is actually filtered seawater.

2

How big?

Scientific name
Protoreaster linckii

Where
Indian Ocean and Central Pacific Ocean

Eats
Soft coral, sponges, tubeworms, clams, mussels, other starfish

Predators
Birds, fish and sea otters

Lifespan
Thirty-five years

Clownfish get their name from their bright orange colouring and white stripes, and from the bouncy way in which they swim. They live alongside anemones, eating their waste matter and uneaten food, as well protecting the anemones from predators.

Clownfish

CLOWNFISH

TOP TRUMPS

Size (cm)	11
Defences	7
Under Threat	0
Depth	85

When a female Clownfish dies, a male has the ability to change gender and take her role!

1

Well, I'm sure YOU didn't know that all clownfish are born male but as they grow older some will change into females!

Protection from Poison
Sea anemones are poisonous but the clownfish is covered with a film of mucus which makes it immune to their nasty sting.

Popular Pets
As a result of the popular movie, *Finding Nemo*, so many people wanted a clownfish as a pet that the wild clownfish population fell by 75%!

Scientific name
Members of the Amphiprioninae family (there are thirty different species)

Where
The warmer waters of the Indian and Pacific Oceans

Eats
Anemone leftovers - algae, plankton, molluscs

Lifespan
Three to six years

Predators
Sharks, stingrays and other large fish, but humans offer the greatest threat

How big?

As soon as a **great white shark** is born, it swims away from its mother who sees it only as prey! And with good reason – sharks will try to eat anything and everything they find. After a good meal, though, a great white shark can go for three months before it starts to feel hungry again.

Great White Shark

Top of the Food Chain
Sharks have been around for some 350 million years. Sharks are apex predators – that means they are at the top of the food chain! They don't have a skeleton made of bone. Instead, their shape is made from cartilage, the same stuff that our noses and ears are made of!

Sixth Sense
As well as having acute hearing and good eyesight, sharks possess an amazing sixth sense called electroreception. This allows them to locate things in the water by sensing the electrical fields they give off.

GREAT WHITE SHARK

TOP TRUMPS

Size (cm)	600
Defences	49
Under Threat	3
Depth	62

Great Whites are one of the largest predators in the world, and their mouths contain over 300 serrated teeth!

Great White Shark beats Manatee on Size, Defences, and Depth!

Great whites have the strongest smell out of all sharks and can smell one drop of blood in a million drops of water. Incredible, but true!

3

How big?

Scientific name
Carcharodon carcharias

Where
In warm open seas and oceans all over the world

Eats
Large fish (including other sharks), dolphins, seals and sea birds

Lifespan
Thirty plus years

Predators
Only orca, the killer whale

The **manatee**, also known as the Sea Cow, lives in marshy coastal regions and will also venture upstream in rivers. Like whales and dolphins, manatees are mammals and they regularly need to come to the water's surface to breathe air.

Manatee

MANATEE

TOP TRUMPS

Size (cm)	335
Defences	2
Under Threat	3
Depth	15

Manatees are large aquatic mammals, nicknamed "Sea Cows". They feed on underwater grass, algae and weeds.

Manatee Teeth
The manatee only has twelve teeth, six on each jaw, but they are replaced continually throughout its lifetime. Its teeth are located at the side of its mouth because it chews its food. The manatee is the only aquatic mammal that is a herbivore (plant-eater).

Bony Flippers
Manatees have bones in their flippers that are like our hands. The bones enable them to move through the water, bring food towards their mouths and also to hold objects. They even have 'finger' nails on each flipper!

0

Well, even more incredibly, the manatee is the source of the mermaid legends! The stories come from hearing manatees 'sing' in the dark.

Scientific name
Trichechus family (there are three different species)

Lifespan
Sixty plus years

Where
Caribbean Sea, Gulf of Mexico, Amazon Basin and West Africa

Eats
Mainly plants and algae

Predators
Whales, sharks, crocodiles and alligators

How big?

Dinner Time!

The great white shark is hungry. Having missed out on a school of tuna fish earlier, he now sees a lone manatee. Frightened, a manatee can swim at 20 mph. The great white is faster and will be able to catch the manatee in the time it takes for it to swim two miles. How long will it take the great white to catch its dinner?

WHAT AM i?

Player 1 looks at the top card on his deck and Player 2 has to work out what the creature is. Player 2 can ask a maximum of five questions which can only be answered with 'YES' or 'NO' answers. If Player 2 guesses correctly within five questions, she takes the card from Player 1 and adds it to her deck. If Player 2 gets it wrong she has to hand over the top card from her own deck. The object is to capture all the cards!

Food Chain

Fish have been on the Earth for 450 million years! That means they were alive long before dinosaurs roamed the earth!

The ocean is a complicated eco-system with apex predators at the top of the food chain. Can you divide the box below into six separate sections so that each section contains an orca, a basking shark, a clownfish and some anemones? We've done the first one for you.

The **Humboldt penguin** is also known as the Peruvian penguin as it is mainly seen off the coast of Peru and Chile in South America. It was named after the German scientist, Alexander von Humboldt, who first explored the area in 1799.

Humboldt Penguin

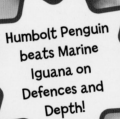

Humbolt Penguin beats Marine Iguana on Defences and Depth!

HUMBOLDT PENGUIN

TOP TRUMPS

Size (cm)	60
Defences	12
Under Threat	3
Depth	70

Humboldt Penguins have a special gland that allows them to drink both fresh and sea water, filtering out excess salt.

Salting Away
Like humans, Humboldt penguins cannot cope with too much salt in their system. They have a special gland which flushes salt out of their body, allowing them to drink salty seawater freely.

Did you know that Humboldt penguins burrow and create nesting sites in 'guano'? That's seabird poo to you and me!

2

Finding Families
Each Humboldt penguin has a distinctly different voice; this allows parents and their offspring to find each other in a crowd.

How big?

Scientific name
Spheniscus humboldti

Where
Pacific coast of South America

Lifespan
Fifteen years in the wild, but can live as long as thirty years in captivity

Eats
Krill and small fish such as anchovies and sardines

Predators
Seals, sharks and killer whales

The **marine iguana** is a rare creature. It is the only known marine lizard in the world, and like so many of the creatures living on the Galapagos Islands, cannot be found anywhere else in the world! They might look fierce, but they're actually gentle herbivores.

Marine Iguana

MARINE IGUANA

TOP TRUMPS

Size (cm)	150
Defences	3
Under Threat	3
Depth	5

Marine Iguanas sneeze regularly to remove salt from their noses!

Warning Sign
The marine iguana's best friend is the Galapagos mockingbird because it lets out a distinctive cry if there is a hawk on the hunt in the area. Any iguana that overhears the alarm will know to escape the approaching danger!

Sun Bathers
Iguanas lie in the sun all day because they are cold blooded. They need the sun's rays to stay warm and help digest food.

1

Well, did you know that marine iguanas can hold their breath for an amazing forty-five minutes?

Scientific name
Amblyrhynchus cristatus

Where
Galapagos Islands

Lifespan
Five to twelve years in the wild

Eats
Seaweed and algae

Predators
Galapagos Hawk and other birds

How big?

It's All in The Name

Read these clues and write the answers in the grid below. Can you find the hidden word?

1 Has something in common with scorpions

2 This creature uses abandoned shells as its home

3 Only one marine version of this animal exists in the world

4 The killer whale

5 One of the fastest fish in the ocean

6 Found off the coast of Japan

7 Common _ _ _ _, also known as Harbour

8 Humboldt or Peruvian

PREDICT TO WIN

Each player's deck of cards is placed face down in a pile. Player 1 takes the top card from her pile (without showing it to the other player) and chooses a category. Player 2 predicts if his top card will win or lose in that category then turns it over. If Player 2 is correct, he adds both cards to the bottom of his pile. If he's wrong, the cards are taken by Player 1.

Aquatic QUiZ

How much have you found out about creatures of the deep? Test your knowledge here!

Over 1,000 species of fish are currently threatened by extinction!

1. An _____ has eight arms.

2. The largest male orca whale weighed a hefty _____ kg!

3. There are more than _____different species of hermit crab.

4. Turtles have been on the endangered species list since 1978. The greatest threats to their survival are _____ , _____, and_____.

5. _____ have no stomach so they need to eat constantly!

6. _____ take possession of empty shells.

7. Ocean water is too _____ for dolphins to drink!!

8. The _____ is the deepest known area of Earth's oceans.

9. _____ of the earth's surface is covered in water!

10. The Japanese spider crab has _____ in its stomach!

11. _____ are the fastest fish in the ocean and can swim at speeds of up to 60 miles per hour!

Answers

Page 8 - Gone Fishing

```
A F I S H A R K B R P A K H
N I F H T T A B R A P U H R
I J S F S T I N G R A Y Y A R
I H H T T W C A F H R B A A
P P G U I A R N I P G R B I
L E E S W O R D F I S H A P
O N L N G U I F B R B C R E
O G T P E N C R I P S H C N
B A R C R E D I P S P O T S
P B U G N I B G R C H P I I
G E T N G E P U F F G A M H
C L P E M A N A T E E E R E
P O W C L O W N F I S H E K
C P L P W P E A G I P S H A
```

The missing word is penguin!

Page 9 - In Danger

Loggerhead Turtle 4
Iguana 3
Octopus 2
Mantis Shrimp 1
Orca Whale 0

Page 14 - Spot the Difference

Page 15 - Shark Attack

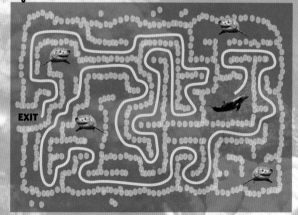

Page 20 - Finding Nemo

36 Clownfish

Page 21 - Ocean Floor

A: Loggerhead Turtle 19
B: Orca Whale 42
C: Starfish 87
D: Stingray 9
E: Anglerfish 94
F: Basking Shark 8

Page 26 - Dinner Time!

Manatee swims 1 mile in 3 minutes (20 mph ÷ 60 minutes), therefore it will take the great white shark 6 minutes to catch its dinner!

Page 27 - Food Chain

Page 30 - It's All in The Name

HIDDEN WORD: SEAHORSE

```
            S T I N G R A Y
        H E R M I T C R A B
    I G U A N A
O R C A W H A L E
    S W O R D F I S H
S P I D E R C R A B
        S E A L
    P E N G U I N
```

Page 31 - Aquatic QUIZ

1. OCTOPUS
2. 10,000 kg!
3. 500
4. POLLUTION, HUMAN ACTIVITIES IN THEIR NESTING AREAS and FISHING NETS.
5. SEAHORSES
6. HERMIT CRABS
7. SALTY
8. MARIANA TRENCH
9. 70%
10. TEETH
11. SWORDFISH